margaret Tempest.

THE KNOT
SQUIRREL TIED

Little Grey Rabbit Books

SQUIRREL GOES SKATING
WISE OWL'S STORY
LITTLE GREY RABBIT'S PARTY
THE KNOT SQUIRREL TIED
FUZZYPEG GOES TO SCHOOL
LITTLE GREY RABBIT'S CHRISTMAS
MOLDY WARP THE MOLE
HARE JOINS THE HOME GUARD
LITTLE GREY RABBIT'S WASHING DAY
WATER RAT'S PICNIC
LITTLE GREY RABBIT'S BIRTHDAY
THE SPECKLEDY HEN
LITTLE GREY RABBIT TO THE RESCUE (*Play*)
LITTLE GREY RABBIT AND THE WEASELS
GREY RABBIT AND THE WANDERING HEDGEHOG
LITTLE GREY RABBIT MAKES LACE
HARE AND THE EASTER EGGS
LITTLE GREY RABBIT'S VALENTINE
LITTLE GREY RABBIT GOES TO THE SEA
HARE AND GUY FAWKES
LITTLE GREY RABBIT'S PAINT BOX
GREY RABBIT FINDS A SHOE
GREY RABBIT AND THE CIRCUS
GREY RABBIT'S MAY DAY
HARE GOES SHOPPING
LITTLE GREY RABBIT'S PANCAKE DAY

Illustrated by Katherine Wigglesworth
LITTLE GREY RABBIT GOES TO THE NORTH POLE
FUZZYPEG'S BROTHER
LITTLE GREY RABBIT'S SPRING CLEANING PARTY
LITTLE GREY RABBIT AND THE SNOW BABY

The Knot
Squirrel Tied

by Alison Uttley
Pictures by
Margaret Tempest

Collins London

FIRST PUBLISHED 1937
FIFTEENTH IMPRESSION 1983
ISBN 0 00 194104 6
COPYRIGHT RESERVED
PRINTED IN GREAT BRITAIN
WILLIAM COLLINS SONS & CO LTD GLASGOW

FOREWORD

OF course you must understand that Grey Rabbit's home had no electric light or gas, and even the candles were made from pith of rushes dipped in wax from the wild bees' nests, which Squirrel found. Water there was in plenty, but it did not come from a tap. It flowed from a spring outside, which rose up from the ground and went to a brook. Grey Rabbit cooked on a fire, but it was a wood fire, there was no coal in that part of the country. Tea did not come from India, but from a little herb known very well to country people, who once dried it and used it in their cottage homes. Bread was baked from wheat ears, ground fine, and Hare and Grey Rabbit gleaned in the cornfields to get the wheat.

The doormats were plaited rushes, like country-made mats, and cushions were stuffed with wool gathered from the hedges where sheep pushed through the thorns. As for the looking-glass, Grey Rabbit found the glass, dropped from a lady's handbag, and Mole made a frame for it. Usually the animals gazed at themselves in the still pools as so many country children have done. The country ways of Grey Rabbit were the country ways known to the author.

ONE MORNING RAT came to his house door and gazed up and down with a weary eye. Then he slowly hobbled out to the hazel spinney and made a crutch to help himself along.

Mrs. Rat shut the door after him, and sighed as she rocked the wicker cradle in which her baby lay.

"Hush-a-bye," she sang in a high shrill voice.

"Father Rat will bring thee an egg,
    He'll either steal or borrow or beg."

"ALAS!" she sighed. "It has never been the same since he stole the food from Grey Rabbit's house, and that *impident* Squirrel tied a knot in his tail. No one can untie it! Poor Rat! He has indeed suffered for his misdoings!"

The little Rat wailed even louder than ever, and his mother shook him till his teeth rattled like ivory bells.

"Hush-a-bye," she sang.

Rat crept along under the shadow of the wall. No longer could he scamper in a light-hearted way with his tail rippling behind him. Now it always dragged in the heavy knot which Squirrel had tied to remind him of his wickedness. The knot was always in the way. It got entangled in briars. No longer could he poach or thieve or hunt.

"EVERY DAY I GET THINNER and thinner, I never can get a really good dinner," Rat told his friends at the Cock and Bull Inn.

HE THOUGHT OF THIS as he sidled along by the wall. At last he reached the farm buildings, and he climbed up the narrow stair into the hen-house. He knew the Speckledy Hen had laid an egg, for he had heard her cackling triumphantly, boasting to all the world, in her silly way, of her cleverness.

Rat crept through the little door and went to the nests. In one lay the big

brown egg, which had the golden yolk
Rat loved so much. He tucked it
under his body, but when he started
downstairs the knot in his tail caught
in the doorway, and he overbalanced.
At that moment the Speckledy Hen
looked up from the farmyard below.
She saw her precious egg clutched in
the arms of the stumbling Rat, and she
set up such a screech that a farm man
ran to the door.

"MY EGG! OH! My dear egg!"
she shrieked.

Rat struggled to get free, and dropped
the egg. It rolled down the stairway
and split on the ground, and Rat rushed
to safety followed by clods of earth and
sticks and stones.

" So near, and yet so far," he groaned,
as he rubbed his sore shins and rested
in a hole in the wall.

He waited till the noise had died
down, which was a long time, for the
Speckledy Hen talked loudly about it
all morning.

" Thinner and thinner and thinner,"
moaned Rat, as he buckled his belt
more tightly and slouched round the
corner.

He crept into the barn where a
fine bag of meal stood in a corner.

HERE was a lucky find! He gnawed a hole in the sack, and had just started to eat the sweet delicious grain, when in his excitement he moved clumsily, and the knot in his tail thumped on the boards.

Bang! Like a drum it sounded, and into the room came the farmyard cat, with her eyes gleaming, and her large mouth wide open.

What a race Rat had for the door! How his tail thumped behind him! He only just got safely away, with his coat torn, and his felt hat left behind in the cat's claws!

" That was a near squeak," said he to a friend, as he mopped his brow, but the other rat only laughed and ran away.

"THERE'S no sympathy among thieves," grumbled Rat. He pulled his belt still tighter, and sat down to think.

"Hedgehog is a kindly soul," said he to himself. "I'll have a talk with him at milking time. Once I gave him a poached egg for little Fuzzypeg. Alas! Never again shall I poach an egg, I fear, but I will remind him of my past goodness."

He waited all afternoon till Hedgehog came trotting across the field with his yoke across his shoulders, and the couple of milk pails jingling-jangling on the chains.

The Rat watched Hedgehog milk a cow and turn away with the warm milk frothing in his little pails. He licked his lips hungrily and then stepped softly after.

OLD HEDGEHOG heard the thump of the tail, and exclaimed, without turning round, " Is that you, Rat? Keep away from my milk pails."

" Hedgehog, Mr. Hedgehog, Sir Hedgehog," said Rat humbly. " A word with you, Sir. A word in your ear, Sir."

Hedgehog put down the pails and waited.

" I'm getting very thin," said the Rat. " I never get anything to eat nowadays."

" Yes," said Hedgehog. " We have all been more comfortable lately."

" I'm as thin as a lath," Rat went on, wiping his eyes with a ragged handker-chief. " I'm nearly a skellington."

" What do you want me to do, Rat? I'll give you a drink of milk if you like."

THE KINDLY HEDGEHOG
held out a pail and Rat drank it all
up with eager gulps.

Hedgehog looked cross. "Now
you've been and done it!" he grumbled. "That was the milk for your
own family, and for Grey Rabbit, and
Hare and Squirrel. I shall have to go
back to the cowshed, and the cow
will be much annoyed."

"Please, kind Hedgehog," whined
Rat, as the Hedgehog turned back to
the cowhouse. "Do give me some
advice. Everyone knows how wise
you are."

"First time I've been called wise,"
said Hedgehog.

"How can I get the knot undone,
Hedgehog?" asked Rat.

"Let me look at it," said the Hedgehog. "Let me see what I can do.

MY FINGERS are all thumbs, but I'll use my prickles."

Rat shivered. "Oh! Oh! Oh-oo-ooh!" he squealed, as the Hedgehog pulled and tugged at the knot with his spikes.

"I can't undo it, Rat. Clever fingers fastened it. Who was it, Rat?"

"It was Squirrel," said Rat. "Well, you'd better ask Squirrel to unfasten it," said Hedgehog.

"It's no use," said the Rat. "If I go near the little house at the end of the wood, they hear me coming, and they bolt the doors."

Hedgehog pondered. "Go and ask Mole's advice," said he. "Tell him I sent you. Once you gave my little Fuzzypeg an egg. It was a bad one, it's true, but still, it was a present."

IT WAS a weary road to Mole's house, with never a vestige of food to be seen in the fields. There were buttercups, but no butter, blackberry-flowers, but no blackberries.

"How I wish I had never gone to Grey Rabbit's larder," said the Rat, as he tramped up the field and crawled under the gate.

There was Mole's house, with Mole digging up pig-nuts in his garden.

As Rat walked up to the door, Mole put down his spade, rubbed his hands on his handkerchief, and then looked round to see if any of his valuables were lying about. One could never be too careful with Rat.

"Good afternoon, Rat," said he. "May I ask what brings you here?"

"PLEASE, MOLE, can you untie the knot in my tail?" asked the Rat, in a tiny, sad little voice. "Hedgehog sent me to you."

Without a word Mole trotted indoors, and returned with a bowl of soup and a slice of bread.

"Eat this," said he. "Then I will look at the knot."

Rat thanked him and gobbled up the food. Then Mole seized the knot with his long pink fingers and struggled and tugged, but still the knot wouldn't come undone.

"It's Squirrel's tying," said he, "but I don't think even her clever fingers could undo this knot. The only one who can help you is Wise Owl."

"**I** DAREN'T GO TO HIM," said Rat shortly. "I'm scared of him. A thin rat would be nothing to a hungry owl."

"Nothing venture, nothing win," replied Mole. "Take him a present, Rat, something special."

"I haven't got a present," said Rat to himself. "I am so poor, I have nothing." He put his hand in his pocket and brought out the ragged handkerchief and a bone. He looked at the bone for a few minutes and then laughed softly.

"I haven't even a knife, but my teeth are sharp, as sharp as a razor. They will do the job."

HE SAT DOWN ON A LOG and gnawed at the bone. He bit a piece off here, and a slip off there, and a snippet from one end, and a whiff from the other, working away, polishing, and rubbing as he went. He was so much interested in his work that night came before he had finished, and he took home his carving.

"HAVE YOU BROUGHT any food, Rat?" asked his wife, when she opened the door. "We've had nothing but vegetable soup to-day, and the milk, which came very late."

"Nothing, wife," said Rat, "but to-morrow I'm going to see Wise Owl.

I'VE HOPES, my dear, hopes! "
He showed his wife his bone and
she sat admiring it as he continued his
work.   Even the baby Rat stopped
crying and began to laugh when he
saw what his father was making.

IT WAS a white little ship with rigging and sails, and tiny portholes. There was a figurehead at the prow, a seagull with outstretched wings.

" How did you think of it? " asked the admiring Mrs. Rat. " I never knew you were so clever, Rat."

" Desperation! " said Rat grimly. " I saw ships a-sailing, long ago. When I was young I went for a voyage in one, but the food wasn't good, and I gave up that wandering life."

" Has it got a name, your white ship? " asked Mrs. Rat.

" I think I'd better call it ' The Good Hope,' " replied Rat.

THE NEXT DAY Rat set off with his finished ship in his pocket, and a clean handkerchief. It had taken him all morning to complete his work, but he had added some delicate carving to the sides. The billowing sails were nearly transparent with his polishing, and the ropes were like cobwebs. He forgot his hunger as he worked, and quite enjoyed himself.

"Work isn't such a bad thing," he told his wife. "I've never done any before." He whistled a cheerful tune.

ON HIS WAY to Wise Owl's wood he had to pass little Grey Rabbit's cottage. Delicious smells came from the window, and Rat crept up to see what was being cooked. He didn't want to get to Owl's house till dusk, so there was plenty of time, and perhaps he might pick up a morsel of food, if he was careful.

Little Grey Rabbit and Squirrel were making tartlets. Grey Rabbit rolled out the pastry with her little rolling-pin, and Squirrel lined the patty-pans ready for the raspberry jam.

"GREY RABBIT, GREY RABBIT," called Hare, running up the garden path and bursting into the kitchen. Rat hid under the juniper bush in the shadow, and Hare passed him without noticing.

" Grey Rabbit and Squirrel," said he. " Haymaking has begun. Daisy Field is cut. Can we all go and play in the hayfield? The grass will be hay by to-morrow with this sunshine."

" Oh, let's," cried Grey Rabbit, and she waved her rolling-pin excitedly. " We'll go when the men have gone home to-morrow evening."

" I KNOW a corner where we can make hay all by ourselves, with no frogs and field-mice to bother us," said Squirrel, absent-mindedly putting the jam into her own mouth instead of into the patty-pans

" We'll invite Mole and Hedgehog and Fuzzypeg to join us," said little Grey Rabbit, " and we'll have tea in the hayfield."

" I'll make some treacle toffee to take with us," said Hare. He took a saucepan and measured out butter and treacle and sugar. He stirred it over the fire, getting in Squirrel's way, and knocking over the flour bin. Then he ran to the garden for a pinch of lavender and sweetbriar and lad's-love, to give it a flavour. Rat held his breath. It was lucky he was as thin as a shadow, or Hare would have seen him.

" That isn't treacle toffee! " exclaimed Squirrel indignantly.

" No, I've changed its name," said Hare, grinning. " It's Lavender Toffee." He stirred in his herbs, and the sweet smell came into the room.

LITTLE GREY RABBIT put her tartlets in the oven, and Hare set his toffee on the window-sill to cool. Then they all went out in the garden and sat among the flowers, sipping lemonade, and fanning themselves with the leaves of the sycamore-tree.

Rat crept up to the back door, and looked into the cosy kitchen. He knew his way about quite well.

" Ah! " he sighed, and he dragged his unwilling tail over the doorway. " I'm safe for a few minutes," said he.

He crouched down by the fire, and sniffed the savoury smells of raspberry tartlets which came from the oven. He opened the oven door and poked his nose in the hot jam.

" Oh! " he squeaked in a muffled voice. " Too hot! "

HE dipped the tip of his tail in the cooling toffee, but that was too hot, also. He squirmed round and looked at the burn. The knot seemed tighter than ever.

Through the open window he heard the three friends make plans for the picnic.

" There's my chance," said Rat. " I'll come along to-morrow and see what I can find. Now I'll go and have a word with Wise Owl."

He looked again at his little ship, white as ivory, and pretty as a picture. Then he shuffled out of the house, and went through the wood to Wise Owl's house in the great beech-tree. He rang the little silver bell which hung from the door, and the sleepy bird came to see who wanted him in the daylight.

RAT waved his handkerchief, and the Owl made a truce. " Rat! " said he gruffly. " What do you want? "

" I've brought you a present, Wise Owl." Rat spoke in a trembling voice.

Wise Owl sat waiting, with his large round eyes staring at the unfortunate rat, whilst Rat fumbled in his pocket and brought out the little ship.

" Hm-m," said Wise Owl, flying down and examining it. " A nice bit of carving. Pity you don't do more work, Rat. Why not try to work instead of to thieve? "

" Please, Wise Owl, will you un-knot my tail? " asked Rat, holding up his paws in a supplicating way. " I am as thin as a leaf, and no one is clever enough to unknot me."

OWL hummed to himself, and turned the tiny bone ship over and over.

"I'm afraid you are still a thief, Rat. What about Speckledy Hen's egg?

"What about the farmer's corn? Where did that jam come from, which I see on your nose? And the treacle toffee on the end of your tail?"

Rat fidgeted uneasily. What keen eyes had Owl!

"The knot will stay tied until you turn over a new leaf, Rat. No one can unfasten it. Turn over a new leaf!"

Owl shut his door and went back to his library, holding the little ship in his claws. He took down his book on sailing-ships, and examined the rigging.

"Quite correct in every detail," said he.

RAT hobbled painfully back through the wood, turning all the green leaves he could reach, but still his tail remained knotted. However, he felt happier, for he had made something, and Owl had looked pleased with it.

The next day, as usual, he paid his visit to the farmyard, to see what he could pilfer. He walked up to the hen-roost and there was the Speckledy Hen's latest egg. Rat looked at it with longing eyes. Speckledy Hen was a good-natured silly creature. He would leave her egg. There would be raspberry tartlets at Grey Rabbit's house.

He turned away and started to go down the stair.

Was it imagination? He felt a loosening in his tail. The knot thumped less noisily as he slid down.

"CLUCK! CLUCK!" cried the Speckledy Hen when she saw him. "Shoo, Rat! Shoo! Have you eaten my egg to-day, as you are not carrying it?" She ran shrieking to her precious egg. There it was, safe and sound! She couldn't understand, and she clucked softly to herself, "Did Rat forget it, or has he turned over a new leaf?"

Rat went into the barn. There was a litter on the floor, and he seized a bunch of twigs and swept it away. Up and down the stones he went, sweeping softly, with scarcely a glance at the meal bag, until the floor was clean. Then he went up to the sack and gazed at its bulging sides.

A pity to mess up the floor again! There would be raspberry tartlets waiting for him. He turned away, and another little hitch in his tail seemed to be loosened.

He went to Hedgehog's house under the hedge.

"Can I do any little thing for you, Hedgehog?" he asked.

Old Hedgehog stared. "Do you mean a little burglary?" he asked.

"No. I'll help to carry your milk pails to the neighbours," said Rat.

"And drink the milk, like you did yesterday," replied the Hedgehog indignantly.

"Try me," said Rat, so Hedgehog trusted him with the milk for the Red Squirrel who lived up in the pine-tree. Hedgehog never liked taking milk to the Red Squirrel, who was so full of jokes, the staid old milkman didn't know what to make of him.

" 'TWILL give him a fright," thought Hedgehog. " Then maybe he'll be more polite to me. Once he sent an old-laig egg to Fuzzypeg! "

So Rat took the milk to the Red Squirrel's door, and knocked gently. He filled the jug at the foot of the tree, and turned away.

"OH!" shouted the Red Squirrel. "A Rat! A Rat!" He fled to the top of his tree, and sat there peeping down. When Rat was out of sight he crept down again, and looked around. His pyjamas, hanging on the clothes-line, were still there; his bowl of nuts was untouched ; the milk-jug was filled to the brim!

RAT walked through the fields. Both his heart and his tail felt lighter, and when he got back to Hedgehog's house, there was a mug of milk and a hunch of bread and cheese, waiting for him on the doorstep.

Fuzzypeg peeped round the corner, all ready to run away. Rat put his hand in his pocket and brought out a dozen oak-apples, which he gave to the astonished little hedgehog for marbles.

As evening came there were sounds of gaiety in the hayfield. In the far corner Squirrel and little Grey Rabbit in blue sun-bonnets were raking the hay, and Hare was piling it up into haycocks. Hedgehog and Fuzzypeg came to help and tossed it with their prickles. Then Mole joined them, with a little hayfork which he had made.

RAT stood looking at the happy scene—an outsider who mustn't venture near. He was on his way to Grey Rabbit's house, where he hoped to find the raspberry tartlets waiting for him. He wouldn't be caught this time! He knew his way about, and Squirrel was safe for an hour or two.

THEN he noticed the feast spread out under the hedge, not far from him. There it lay, in the shade of the foxgloves, with no one to guard it! There was a little white cloth and on it a basket filled with the tempting raspberry tartlets! So it was of no use to go to the house, for the food was here!

THERE WERE nut leaves laden with wild strawberries and raspberries, and a jug full of cream. There was crab-apple jelly, and sloe jam, little green lettuces, and radishes like rosebuds, and a big plum cake, and the treacle toffee!

Rat's mouth watered. He stared so hard at the plum cake that he felt he could taste its delicious sugary crust. Then he turned away and walked home.

A great pink cloud like a bunch of roses lay in the sky, and swifts cut across the blue air. Rat gazed up at the birds, so light and free, and at that moment he felt light and free, too.

THE LAST KNOT in his tail had come undone. He was a happy rat, loosened from his fetters, and he ran home to tell his wife, whisking his tail like a whip around his head.

" I saw Rat staring at our feast," confided Grey Rabbit to the others as they sat round in a circle among the foxgloves. " He didn't touch a thing, and he didn't know that I saw him."

" He was reminded of his past wickedness by the knot in his tail," said Squirrel, as she munched the nuts and strawberries ; " and I tied that knot. It will never, never come undone."

"RAT helped to carry my milk to-day, and when I went to the barn he had swept it clean," said old Hedgehog.

"Rat gave me some marbles," cried little Fuzzypeg.

"He seems a changed animal," said little Grey Rabbit.

"I wonder if Wise Owl gave him some good advice," mused the Mole.

The next morning Rat came to little Grey Rabbit's house. He carried a pair of shears and a scythe instead of his club and gun. He was neat and tidy, and he walked with a quick light step.

"CAN I gather your firewood, Grey Rabbit? " said he. " Can I mow your lawn, or cut your hedge, or weed your garden? "

" Why! The knot has gone from your tail, Rat! " exclaimed Grey Rabbit. " Who untied it, Rat? "

" No one," replied Rat modestly. " It came undone by itself. I'm not a thief any more. I understand now what Wise Owl meant when he told me to turn over a new leaf. I shall work for my living, little Grey Rabbit."

He took up his shears and cut the hedge, making peacocks and balls and ships. He mowed the lawn smooth as silk.

HE WENT in the wood to gather sticks, and as he passed under Owl's tree, the wise bird looked out.

"Ho! Ho!" he hooted. "A reformed Rat. The knot is not! A skilful Rat! An artist! Go on with the good work, Rat, and bring me another present someday. I shall be honoured to accept it."

THE RAT blushed through his dusky skin with pride, but he went on gathering his sticks. When he had a great bundle he carried it to the door of the little house. At night he went home with his wages in his pocket, a respectable working animal.

"I'M GOING to carve something else," said he to his wife. "You've never seen anything like what I'm going to make!" He sat down at the table with his little white bone, and began to carve—but that is a secret for another time!

The End of the Story